WELCOME TO THE

INTERNATIONAL RIDING ACADEMY'S

E-QUEST-RIAN PROGRAM FOR KIDS !

GRADE 4

EQUESTRIAN

ACTIVITY BOOK

3rd edition

To record your equi-tastic adventures
What secrets will you discover?

(Pony Club third D Level equivalency)

Written by Melanie Patton
Illustrated by Melanie and Kaela Patton

~Warning! ~

Attention horse lovers: do not let non-horse-lovers see this book!

HELLO! Watch Video #0

You NEED this book for Grades 2, 3, and 4!
<u>Horses!</u> by Melanie Patton
Order from
Amazon.com
This Activity Book is designed to go with the DVD that is only available through the International Riding Academy. Become a member and enjoy the benefits.

Membership is for Sept. 1 – Aug. 31.

Equestrian-4-Kids Overview: 12 units of 5 lessons (15-60 minutes average). Grades follow age/average reading skill as per the school system.

- **Pre-K** – 4 years old – purely for fun & development
- **Kindergarten** – 5 years old – purely for fun & development
- **Grade 1** – 6 years old - purely for fun & development
- **Grade 2** - 7 years old   (Equivalent to Pony Club first D level)
- **Grade 3** - 8 years old   (Equivalent to Pony Club second D level)
- **Grade 4** - 9 years old   (Equivalent to Pony Club third D level)
- **Grade 5** - 10 years old (Equivalent to Pony Club first C level)
- **Grade 6** - 11 years old (Equivalent to Pony Club second C level)
- **Grade 7 -** 12 years old (Equivalent to Pony Club third C level)
- **Grade 8** - 13 years old (Equivalent to Pony Club first B level)
- **Grade 9** - 14 years old (Equivalent to Pony Club second B level)
- **Grade 10 -** 15+ years old (Equivalency to Pony Club H level)

Young Rider Levels are designed to be an added incentive for learning to ride properly with a coach. Young Rider Levels A, B, C and D are perfect before starting with the International Rider Levels. To be based on global set standards, send in a video for grading and completion of each Young Rider Level. A **Young Rider A, B, C or D certificate** will be mailed out after successful completion. This program is free for all members.

Video evaluation is available in equestrian disciplines, based on riding tests/patterns, which must be videoed and sent in for grading, earning **Awards**!

GRADE CHECKLIST	
1	QUIZ SHEET
2	PRESENTATION
3	BOOKS READ
4	HORSE HOURS
5	FIND PROFESSOR'S LOST TOOL WRITE THE PAGE NUMBER HERE
6	FIGURE OUT THE GATE KEEPER'S NAME WRITE THE NAME HERE
7	UNCOVER SECRET UNIT 13

Quests 1 - 4:

1. <u>QUIZ SHEET</u>: Answer all of the questions and mark it. Answers on the website.

2. <u>PRESENTATION PROJECT</u>:
Do one per grade - *For more information on the project presentation topics, see the Lord Chancellor's letter in Unit 8.*

OPTIONAL QUESTS: These numbers are recorded on your certificate.

3. <u>EQUI-BOOKWORM</u>: Record the books you read this year.

4. <u>HORSE HAPPINESS</u>:
Record the hours you spent with a horse this year.

5. <u>BONUS QUEST - RIDING CHALLENGE</u>:

You can earn a special certificate in the Young Rider levels. Have a coach or instructor help you through the checklist, then video the young rider test per level and send it in for grading and awards.
Have fun and remember to smile when you ride!

4

Lord Chancellor Spursnomore
International Riding Academy
Land of Rian
September

Dear Grade 4'er,

I am so excited that you want to learn about horses! I love horses with all my heart and hope you will too.

I have been living in a secret world full of horses, and have learned so much. I have sent some things to the estate and they are in the Grand Hall. Look for them there. I wrote everything in a journal that I call, "HORSES!", and I keep it hidden in the estate library. I left my library card with the butler and you may borrow it until you get your own. But, keep it safe!

Do the activities, complete the quiz sheet and have your teacher mark it. Do a presentation project and finish your special certificate.

You can learn to ride and earn more certificates, ribbons, rosettes, sashes, stall plates, award plaques and more! There are special challenges for reading, and for spending time with horses.

Do not waste any time. The time portal is only open until August 31 for this grade and it is guarded by a gate keeper. Learn his name to travel through to a new world a go on an awesome adventure!

WARNING: the professor's time machine does not always work !
IF YOU GET LOST, FOLLOW THE STORM TO FIND THE VORTEX.
Also, try and find the ancient Mu stones, I believe they hold the secrets of the ancient maps!

L C Spursnomore

CONTENTS:

(This is a fun story that will help lead you to the next grade)

I see you have already started your journey…..

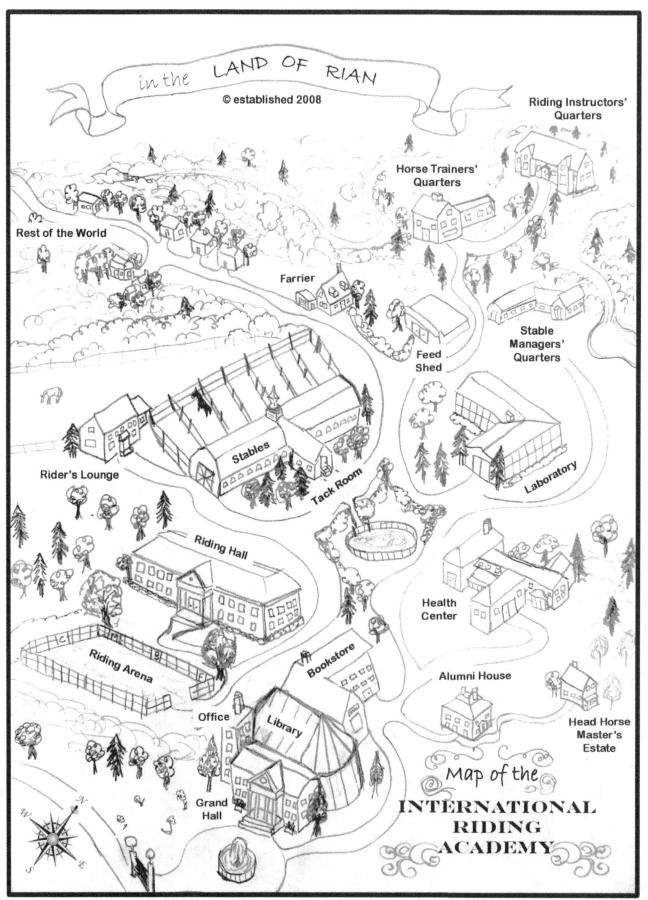

in the LAND OF RIAN

© established 2008

Rest of the World

Riding Instructors' Quarters

Horse Trainers' Quarters

Farrier

Feed Shed

Stable Managers' Quarters

Stables

Rider's Lounge

Tack Room

Laboratory

Riding Hall

Health Center

Riding Arena

Bookstore

Alumni House

Office

Library

Grand Hall

Head Horse Master's Estate

Map of the

INTERNATIONAL RIDING ACADEMY

UNIT 1 HISTORY

Watch Video #1 and Read along

Lesson 1: Introduction

LIBRARY CARD
L.C. Spursnomore

L.C. Spursnomore
Membership Number: S3-0001
Valid until: August 1982
ACCESS UNLIMITED

If found, please return to:

I.R.A. Box 633, Yorkton, SK, S3N 2W7, Canada

Exhausted from your long journey in the heat, you knock on the heavy, wooden doors of the International Riding Academy. It seems like a whole year but, finally, the butler answers. "I've been awaiting your arrival. Your instructor said you would be coming. Welcome back. I was surprised when the master told me you lost your library card and need to borrow his again. Guard it well this time. I shall fetch you a cold drink."

the Butler

When the butler disappeared into one of the many rooms that connected to the Grand Hall, you reach into your shirt pocket and pull out a little pony that fits in the palm of your hand. "Are you okay, Nickers?"

"I feel so hot and exhausted. I need my magic oats," the little pony replied in a whisper of a voice.

"Don't worry Nickers, I see that darn cat!" You tuck him back into your pocket and seek out the sleeping cat. Along your way, you notice several portraits hanging on the wall.

Our Founder

Roper

Cowboy

8

Pioneer

Indian

Conquistador

Calvary

R.C.M.P.

You find the cat sleeping on a couch. Carefully nestled between his front paws is Nickers magic oats. Slipping them out without waking the old, lazy cat, you take the magic oats. "Here Nickers, eat'"

"I feel much better now!" He shook himself off and then something funny happened. Nickers started to grow, not a lot, but just enough to tell a difference.
Examine Nickers a little closer.

"I feel so drained of all my color. Will you color me?"

10

Lesson 2: History

the Librarian

"Nickers, you look fantastic, you even got some color back," you tell Nickers as you make your way to the library.

"It sure does. I shall like to be colored this way", Nickers whinnied with excitement.

"Let's find the library". The two of you travel down the darkened hallway until you see a door that has "Enter at Your Own Risk!" scrawled on it. You push the squeaky door open to see the librarian staring at you.

"Do you have a library card?" You hand over the borrowed card. "Well, this is obviously not your card! It is expired. You look familiar. I will have to make you a new card. Until then you can only browse this section.

You pick up a book that shows many pictures of the 'United States Cavalry' when the army helped tame the Wild West. If you were in the army, you may have to fight in a war and help uphold the peace from the back of a horse. Police, or the Sheriff and his Deputies rode horses to catch the bad guys. In Canada, the police are still called the Royal Canadian Mounted Police. Draw a picture of yourself as either in the Cavalry or as a mounted officer.

Another book explained all about the Indians who were in North America before the settlers came. Once the Spanish Conquistadors came, horses escaped and roamed the countryside. They are called Mustangs. Many native people rode these horses. Look up more pictures and information on their culture and how they rode. What is so special and important about the way they rode their horses?

Lesson 3: Famous Horses

When you finished reading the books, you notice another book on famous horses in television. Here are some names of famous fictional horses.

- Mr. Ed
- Silver who was Lone Ranger's horse
- Scout who was Tonto's horse
- Tornado who was Zorro's horse

Can you think of any more famous television horses? Or even other horses from these television series?

Draw a picture about your favorite famous TV horse. Describe your picture.

Lesson 4: Vocabulary Word Search

Let us start with learning some vocabulary and find the **BOLD** words in the puzzle below.
A **FOAL** is a **BABY HORSE** or **PONY.**
A **COLT** is a **MALE** foal.
A **FILLY** is a **FEMALE** foal.
A **WEANLING** is a colt or filly that is several months old and is weaned.
A **YEARLING** is a colt or filly who is one year old.
A **SIRE** is the baby's **FATHER**.
A **DAM** is the baby's **MOTHER**.

L	N	S	I	C	G	K	E	R
A	S	I	P	O	N	Y	N	E
O	E	R	F	F	I	L	L	Y
F	W	E	A	N	L	I	N	G
E	C	H	T	D	R	S	M	A
M	O	T	H	M	A	L	E	G
A	L	O	E	I	E	■	D	C
L	T	M	R	O	Y	B	A	B
E	S	R	O	H	A	T	M	S

It looks as though the words are forward, backward, up and down. Use the left over letters to fill in the blanks. The words are never repeated within words, such as male and female.

Mystery Quest:
Use the left over letters to spell a phrase. Go left to right, top to bottom. Color in unused letter to help.

—— —— —— —— —— —— —— —— —— —— —— ——

—— —— —— —— —— —— —— —— —— !

Lesson 5: Activity

There is no quiz for this unit; however, there is a quest that will take one year to complete.

The Academy would like to support all equine and equestrian authors. The International Riding Academy's Equestrian Challenge is a contest to see how many books you can read in one year. The year starts with September 1st and lasts until August 31st of the following year, much the same as the school year.

Your quest is to read as many horse related books as you can, and record the number.

At the end of the year, email the office with your number.

It will be recorded on your certificate.

Have fun and dive into a good book, learn about horses and see what adventures you will go on.

That is why the Library door has the sign, "Enter at your own risk!' written on it.

Bonus Activity

Word Search

B	U	C	K	S	K	I	N	X
C	T	X	M	A	R	E	D	E
H	R	X	W	T	X	W	U	G
E	O	G	E	L	D	I	N	G
S	U	R	S	L	X	L	I	A
T	G	E	T	I	H	D	C	S
N	H	Y	R	O	A	N	K	K
U	B	A	R	N	N	X	E	I
T	X	S	H	O	D	X	R	N
S	H	E	L	T	E	R	S	X

Wild
Buckskin
Roan
Gelding
Mare
Dun
Nickers
West
Hand
Gaskin
Chestnuts
Shelters
Barn
Trough
Grey
Shod

16

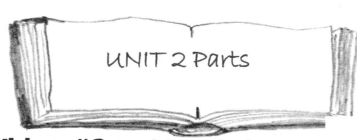

UNIT 2 Parts

Watch Video #2 and Read along
Lesson 1: Parts

"Excuse me, I hate to interrupt, but I want to let you know that your library card is ready," the butler announced.

"Come on, Nickers. With our library card we will be able to enter the library now," you tell the small pony as he hops into your shirt pocket. Once past the library doors you see rows and rows of books. There was

even a balcony for the upper level books. Huge windows draped the ceiling, allowing in light, making it is a little less dark and scary. In the middle of the room was an ornate bookcase encased in glass. It held even more artifacts from the master's journeys. So many books took your breath away.

Not sure where to begin, you try to go up the staircase to get to the second floor, but it is locked by a small gate. The librarian tells you that in order to use the upper wings of the library, you need to use a computer to enter your secret access code and the gate will unlock.

Instead, you look around the main floor of the library. You and Nickers begin scanning book titles and thumbing through the pages of any interesting books. "Lord Chancellor Spursnomore's journal must be here somewhere," you think aloud.

"Maybe it's in that fancy bookcase?" Nickers whispers.

The two of you stroll over to the enlightened bookcase. There were dozens of drawings, scrolls, figurines, books and even a model of a horse skeleton! On the very bottom shelf, tucked away in the deepest corner was a wooden box. It looked like it was hand carved and had a burnished gold latch. As you undo the latch the lights flicker in the library. Pausing a moment until the lights stay on, you open the box.

A few moths flutter out. Inside the box was an old book. You carefully take it out and blow the dust off. On the front, carved into the leather were the initials, "LCS".

"We found it!" Nickers said delighted. "This must be Lord Chancellor Spursnomore's secret journal."

Fill in your library card, draw in your picture, your ID number is the same one as your membership number for the International Riding Academy. Cut it out when you are done. Keep it in a safe place.

LIBRARY CARD

.... *signature*

Name: _____

ID #: _____

Valid until: August 31, 20___

ACCESS WING: Grade ____

Professor's Tool on Page #: _____

Gatekeeper's Name:

_____

Protect this card with your life!
If found, please return to:
I.R.A. Box 123, North State, Rian, Innerearth

You look inside and read chapter one.
Outside the sky was growing dark. "Library's closing in fifteen minutes!" the librarian said.
"Nickers, we should try and make some notes."

Read the Introduction, Chapter One and Two in the book titled, "Horses!"

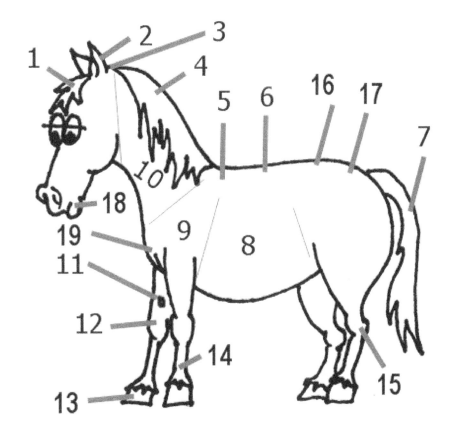

knee _____   ears _____   hoof _____   tail _____

neck _____   poll _____   back _____   withers _____

mane _____   hock _____   fetlock _____   barrel _____

forelock _____   shoulder _____   chestnut _____   muzzle _____

croup _____   loins _____   chest _____

Lesson 2: More Parts

Look up how to measure a horse
Take the total number of inches and divide by four. Find the number of left over inches. Say the number of hands and then the number of inches left over.

For example:
A horse stands 62 inches high.
Divide 62 by 4 = 15 with 2 inches left over.
Therefore the horse is said to be 15-2 hands high or 15.2. We do not use decimals to describe a horse's height, but we say the point. (Confusing isn't it?)

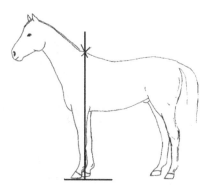

How tall is your horse?

If you were a horse, how tall would you be?

How many hands high is your parent or riding coach?

How tall are you pets or your largest, stuffed teddy bear?

Lesson 3: Awesome Anatomy

Mystery Anatomy: What parts are these? Fill in the blanks.

__ __ __

__ __ __ __

__ __ __ __

__ __ __ __

__ a __ __ __ l

Lesson 4: Activity

Color the horse following the guidelines listed below.

Color the chest pink   Color the hooves purple

Color the muzzle blue   Color the elbow green

Color the loin red   Color the gaskin orange

Color the croup black   Color the forearm brown

"Hold still Nickers, while I see if I can name your parts," you tell the little pony as you start to poke him.
He giggled, "No, no! I'm far too ticklish, go and use a real horse for that!"

**Use your horse and put a sticker on all of the parts you know!
Be sure to take the stickers off when you are done.**

Lesson 5: Quiz

STOP! It would be disastrous to continue without testing your
knowledge each unit.
Do the Quiz for Unit 2.
Color in the dot for the correct answer.
Use your reference book to find the answers.
The quiz sheet is in the back of this book.
When you are done have it marked to earn your certificate.
Answers are on the website.

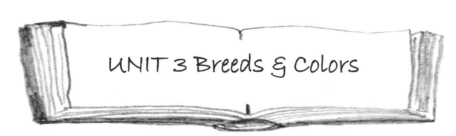

UNIT 3 Breeds & Colors

Watch Video #3 and Read along
Lesson 1: Breeds

The wind howled outside, causing the trees to tremble. The cat was curled up in a ball and sleeping soundly when unexpectedly, there was a loud, piercing whistle coming from somewhere close by outside. The cat screeched and ran from the room. The whistle grew louder and shook the library shelves, rattling all of the books. "What is that?" the librarian yelled.

The butler burst into the room, "It's the professor's machine. He can't stop it and I think it will explode!"

Nickers jumps into your shirt pocket and the two of you run outside. The terrible noise was coming from the laboratory. The professor scrambled like mad adjusting levels, releasing throttles and checking gauges. The laboratory was full of clutter. There were books and papers scattered everywhere.

"Professor, are you ok?" you holler out, covering your ears. He was so busy making adjustments that he didn't hear you. The machine was very interesting with all kinds for buttons, nozzles and instrument gauges. One of the gauge's needles was pointing to a red area and a little light saying, "danger' was flashing on and off. You reach out to hit the off switch, but suddenly the professor was beside you.

"Don't touch anything!" the professor warned, "This dratted wind is wrecking everything, and she could blow at any time!" The professor ambled through switches and gears as you backed away as fast as you could. Within seconds, there was a small explosion and some of the machine's parts fell off, but at least the machine stopped its shrill noise. "There that will do for now," the

the Professor

professor started scrambling around the laboratory trying to gather his papers. You jump up immediately and start grabbing papers to take them into the back room, where it was safe.

"You! I don't remember you, but I need your help. I can't lose all my important papers; you need to organize these papers for me. Just don't go in the front room or touch anything else," the professor warned and then hurried out to put the machine back together.

You begin thumbing through the books and papers, stacking everything in neat little piles. The wind continued to howl and blow things over outside. The professor's angry comments droned in the wind. Guessing he would be quite busy; you get comfortable in a chair next to a lamp and take a little time to read some of his notes.

Read Chapter Three in the book titled, "Horses!"

Put these breeds of horses into the correct category.

Shetland

Arabian   **Types of Light Horses:**

                                           _____

Percheron   _____

                                           _____

Clydesdale

                                           Types of Heavy Horses:

Welsh   _____

                                           _____

Thoroughbred   _____

Quarter horse   **Types of Ponies:**

                                           _____

Shire   _____

                                           _____

Miniature horse

Lesson 2: Colors

Match these definitions with the right color

____ buckskin   1. Golden color with light mane and tail

____ grey   2. Stripe on back, shoulder, and legs

____ flea-bitten grey   3. White hairs mixed in

____ chestnut   4. All black

____ bay   5. The darkest grey

____ steel grey   6. Grey that has red flecks

____ dun   7. Grey that has round, white spots

____ palomino   8. A chocolate colored horse

____ black   9. A reddish brown horse with black points

____ dapple grey   10. A reddish copper colored horse

____ brown   11. Black and white hairs mixed make what color

____ roan   12. Cream color and black points

Lesson 3: Markings

Draw these markings

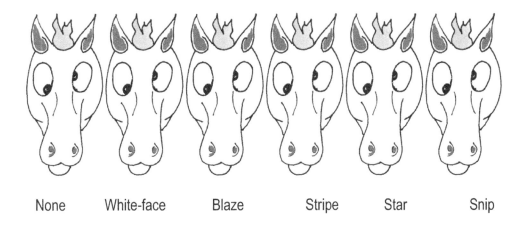

None   White-face   Blaze   Stripe   Star   Snip

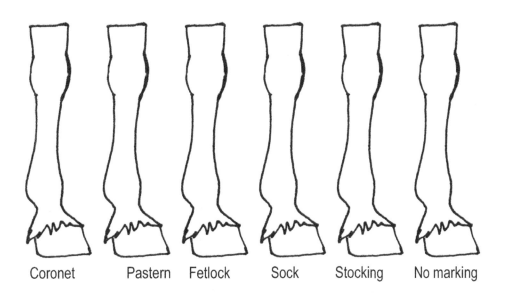

Coronet   Pastern   Fetlock   Sock   Stocking   No marking

Lesson 4: Activity – Your Own Color Chart

Color Nickers in the following color patterns

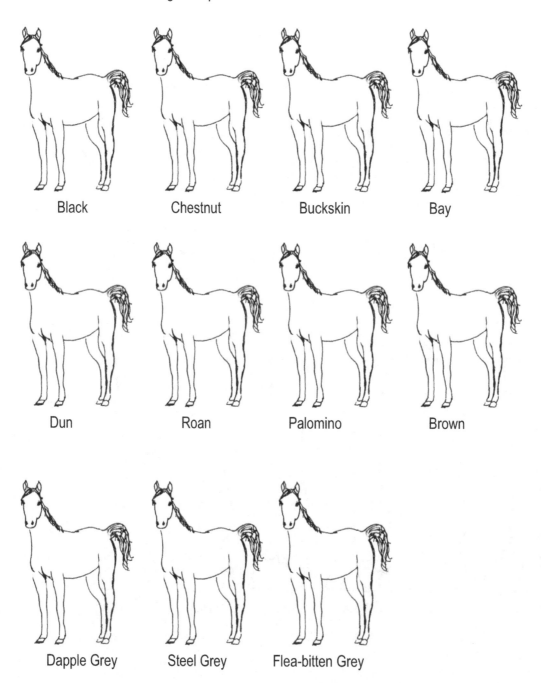

Black	Chestnut	Buckskin	Bay
Dun	Roan	Palomino	Brown
Dapple Grey	Steel Grey	Flea-bitten Grey	

Lesson 5: Quiz

STOP! Colors help define the horse and there are many different breeds to study. It would be crazy to continue without testing your knowledge each unit.
Do the Quiz for Unit 3.

UNIT 4 Hooves

Watch Video #4 and Read along
Lesson 1: The Hoof

You jumped a little when the professor came into the office yelling. "That farrier, he's always taking my tools. I'm too angry to talk to him and I cannot fix my machine without my tool. Go and tell him I want it back!" The professor's face turned red with anger and he was about to storm out. "The tool I want looks like this," he pointed to a diagram on the wall, and then he stormed

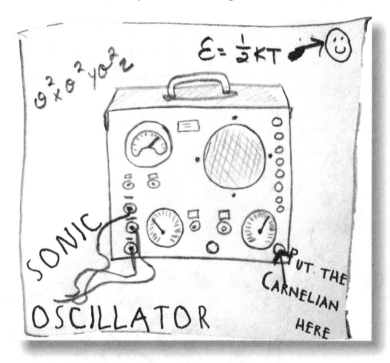

out of the office.

> **Quest: You must keep an eye out for the Professor's lost tool. You can find it somewhere in this book. The professor will need this tool to try and power the machine in the secret Unit 13.**

Clenching the journal in your hand, you walk outside where the winds were blowing even harder than before. You make your way over to the little building with the word "Farrier" written on it. The farrier was standing outside the little, old shed. He wore a leather apron that stored tools in his pockets. He was busy hammering shoes on a horse when you came up and introduced yourself.

"Relieved to see you," he said while pounding another nail. "There's not much time to talk and it's getting far too windy for the fire in my forge, I gotta find some shoes scattered around the shop. Be careful, you should know what you are doing before coming into my shop."

He went back to hammering the nails and the horse quietly stood beside him. You should do some studying before helping the farrier.

Read Chapter Four in the book titled, "Horses!"

COLOR

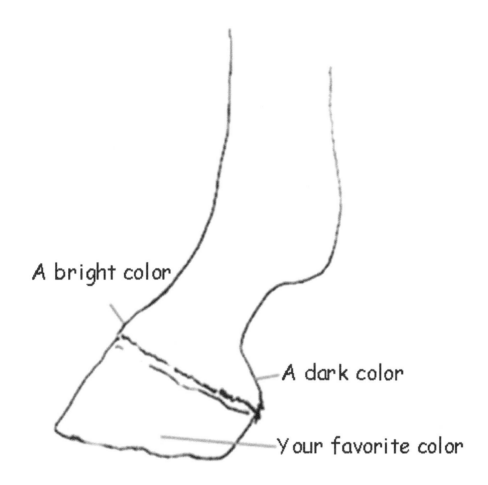

A bright color

A dark color

Your favorite color

32

Lesson 2: Under the Hoof

What number is the correct part of the hoof?

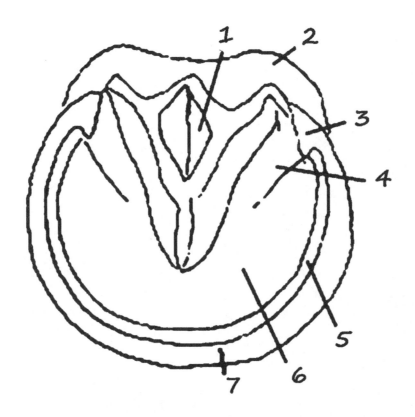

What number is the sole? _____

What number is the hoof wall? _____

What number is the frog? _____

What number is the bar? _____

What number is the heel? _____

What number is the white line? _____

© 2021 International Riding Academy

Lesson 3: Meet the Farrier

What are two things a farrier does to the horse's hooves?

1 _____ & 2 _____

Match the farrier's tools to their correct names.

HAMMER   KNIFE   RASP   NIPPERS

Match the farrier's shoes to their correct names.

HEART BAR   BAR   EGG BAR

Why would you want to shoe a horse?

1) H ____ lp his m__v__ment

2) Help him get a gr__p

What is 1 thing to look for when checking a newly shod foot?

Check new shoes, to _____ that the _____ match!

34

Lesson 4: Activity

How many horse shoes can you find in the picture? Circle each one.
Also: can you find the farrier's tools? He needs the hammer, nippers and rasp.

I found _____ shoes and I found the ___ hammer,
___rasp and ___nippers.

* Practical Activity: Have an instructor or a farrier show you how to pick up a hoof and clean it out properly.

"Thanks for your help," the farrier smiled and shook your hand. "If there's anything I can do for you, just let me know." Thinking now was a good time to ask the farrier about the professor's tool, you ask him for it, but the reply wasn't quite what you were expecting. "I never took no tool!" he said angrily. "That professor, he's always blaming me for his forgetfulness. He leaves his tools all over the estate and never remembers where he left anything!"

"It's ok," you tell him, trying to calm him down, "I will check over there in the stables.

The farrier grumbled and went back to work forging new shoes in the blazing hot fire. "You tell that professor, if I find his tools I'll melt them up and make Nickers some new shoes!"

Nickers whinnied happily from inside your pocket. Waving your hand you turn and head towards the stables. In the middle of the pathways around the estate was a large ring of sand. You decide to crawl through the fence and investigate the sandy area. For fun, you kick up the sand that scattered in the wind. That was when you noticed something odd laying in the sand.

Lesson 5: Quiz

STOP! No hoof, no horse! That means if the horse's hoof or hooves are bad they cannot move or be ridden. It would be disastrous to continue without testing your knowledge each unit.
Do the Quiz for Unit 4.

UNIT 5 Tack

the stablehand

Watch Video #5 and Read along
Lesson 1: Saddles
You reached down to pick up the strange glowing object. It was an orange colored crystal. A man called out to you from the tack room, so you quickly hide the crystal in your pocket.

"You, who are you? Never mind. If you are here to help, you best come inside. I need all of these saddles cleaned, oiled and polished. Then you have to wash all of the saddle pads. Can't have the horses chafing you know," said the older man with dark skin and a cowboy hat.

"I actually came to find a tool for the professor. Have you seen it?"

"Don't have time for the professor and his lost tools. This dusty wind can do a lot of damage to the tack, best to care for it. Help me out then maybe I'll help you out," he said shoving a saddle in your arms.

Read Chapter Five in the book titled, "Horses!"

Western Saddle - The western saddle was designed to help make cowboys more comfortable in the saddle when they had to ride all day. The horn is used for tying a rope to. Match the words to the Western saddle parts.

Horn
Latigo
Fork & Swells
Dee Ring
Keeper

Cantle
Stirrup
Fender
Skirt
Dee for Back Cinch
Stirrup Strap
Seat

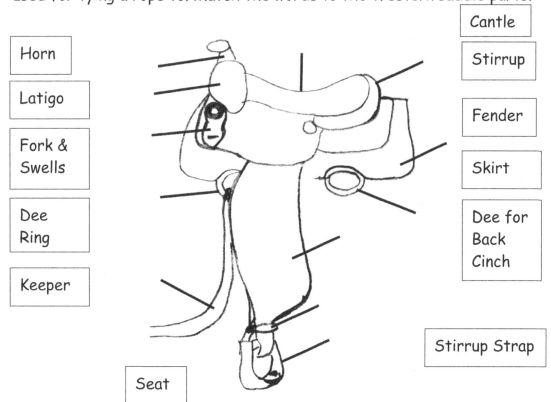

38

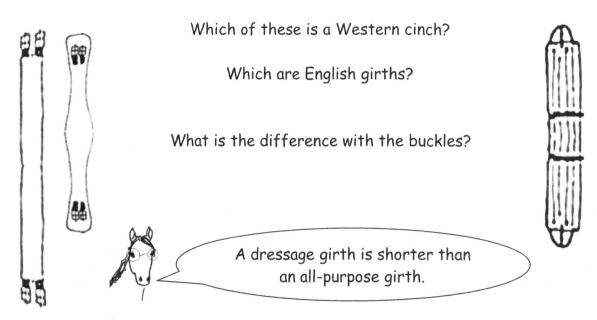

Which of these is a Western cinch?

Which are English girths?

What is the difference with the buckles?

A dressage girth is shorter than an all-purpose girth.

English Saddle - The English saddle is a flat saddle used in many different forms of riding, like Jumping, Eventing, Dressage and Racing. Match the words to the English saddle parts.

| Knee Block | Pommel | Seat | Panel | Flap |

Gullet

Cantle

Stirrup Leather

Buckle Guard

Waist

Skirt

Sweat Flap

Iron

Stirrup Bar

Billets

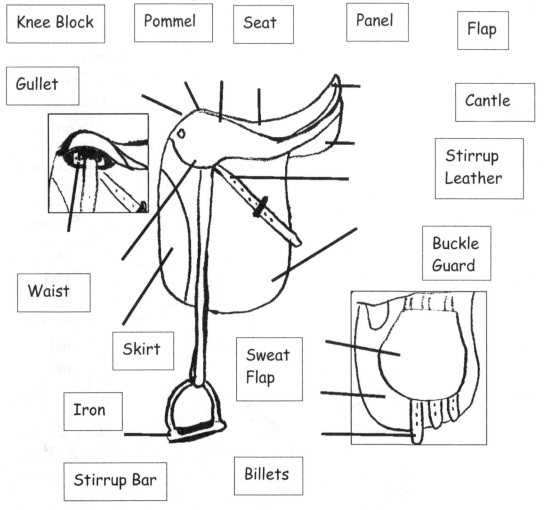

Lesson 2: Bridles & Bits

Color the bridles according to color:

Crown piece = brown   Cheek piece = rose pink
Browband = grey   Reins = navy
Throatlatch = purple   Bit = yellow
Cavesson = burgundy

Bits: Draw a line from the bit to its correct name.

Eggbutt   Dee Ring   Large Ring

Match these cavessons to their correct name

Noseband

Flash

Figure Eight

Crescent

Dropped

What is the purpose of a cavesson?

It _____ the horse's mouth.

Lesson 3: Tack and Care

Mystery Tack: Label the following pieces of mysterious tack.

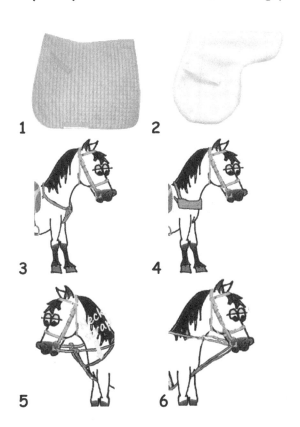

1

2

3

4

5

6

Which is the shaped pad? 1 or 2

Which is the square pad?   1 or 2

Which is the breast plate? 3 or 4

Which is the breast collar? 3 or 4

Which is the standing martingale? 5 or 6

Which is the running martingale? 5 or 6

Order how to clean your tack:

_____ 1. Oil

_____ 2. Take apart

_____ 3. Put together

_____ 4. Wash

42

Lesson 4: Practical Activity

We've come for your tack!

> **TACK ATTACK!**
> Evil germs and dust bunnies are gnawing away at your tack!
> You quest, should you choose to accept it, is to clean your tack.
> This book will self-destruct if you do not.
>
> If you do not want to clean your tack alone, why not invite a friend over or a whole bunch of friends and have a tack cleaning party?

"There, all finished!" you say exhausted. Noticing the logo on each article of tack, you decide to question the stable hand.

"That, there symbol is from the land of Equest Rian. The Queen, herself, granted Lord Chancellor use of that symbol. It became the Academy's logo back in 1898."

"Where is Lord Chancellor now?" you ask, hoping to hear the whole story.

The stable hand shrugged his shoulders, "No one knows for sure. But I betya he's having a great time learning all kinds of things about horses. He stops in here from time to time to oversee how the academy is doing. It's been awhile since his last visit."

"When do you think he'll be back?"

"Can't say for sure, but I can tell you that if you want to be the new apprentice, you had best be on your best behavior and learn all you can about the horses. The Lord Chancellor doesn't have time to spend on slackers." He leaned forward, "Now what was it you wanted again? Oh yes, the professor's tool. I think I saw that in the feed shed. Be careful in there. There's a lot of feed in there and who knows what else."

Lesson 5: Quiz

STOP! Not knowing tack is like not knowing about bait when going fishing. It would be pointless to continue without testing your knowledge each unit.
Do the Quiz for Unit 5.

UNIT 6 Feed

Watch Video #6 and Read along

Lesson 1: Nutrition

You travel back to the feed shed. The wind was really starting to howl now and by the time you got to the building, your ears were ringing from the noisy wind. Glad to be inside, you slam the big door shut, locking out the incessant wind. Groping in the dark for a light switch, you finally flick on the light. A cat hissed and went leaping over the bags of feed and into the hay bales stacked up high.

"If I were a dog, I'd chase that cat," Nickers whinnied from your pocket, "But something smells really good in here."

"Are you hungry, Nickers?" you set him down in front of some lush, green alfalfa hay.

Glancing around the place, you notice some interesting posters on the wall.

Read Chapter Six in the book titled, "Horses!"

Scrambled Oats: Unscramble these words to name a type of feed.

soat _____   ssgra _____

yha _____

paple _____

nimeral _____   waert _____

swtee deef _____ _____

tals _____

Lesson 2: Feed - Can you find out what food each horse likes to eat?
Follow the lines and write your answers on the next page.

Answers:

1. The Arabian horse likes _____

2. The Miniature horse likes _____

3. The dappled grey horse likes _____

4. The Quarter horse likes _____

5. The Appaloosa (polk-a-dots on face too) horse likes

_____

6. The Percheron likes _____

Lesson 3: Feed Management

Fill in the blanks with the following words.

little	oats	bulk	10-12	carrot	pulp
water	apple	clean	feed	sudden	

1. Feed _____ and often.

2. Feed plenty of _____ food every day.

3. Horses should have plenty of clean, fresh _____ available at all times.

4. Feed a treat (succulent) every day, such as a _____ or an

_____.

5. Do not feed lots of _____.

6. Soak beet _____ before feeding it to horses.

7. Keep feed dishes and buckets _____.

8. Make sure to _____ enough.

9. Do not make _____ changes.

10. A horse needs about _____ gallons of water every day.

Lesson 4: Practical Activity

Do up a Feed Schedule for your horse

Time of Day	Feed	Amount
Morning		
Noon		
Evening		
Morning Supplements		
Evening Supplements		
Treats		

Source of Salt: _____

Other: _____

How much does your horse's feed cost?

Date	Feed	Amount

Nicker's Magic Oats Recipe

Magic Oat Cookies

4 cups oat flour
3/4 cup water
1/2 cup diced carrot
4 tbsp blackstrap molasses
1 tbsp oil
1 1/2 tsp salt
Mix well before baking at 350 then top with
1tsp of the magic ingredient –

"Hey, Nickers, look! It's a recipe for some magic oat cookies. Maybe we should make some in case you need some again."

"I can't wait, but- oh, no! The magic ingredient has been ripped off the card!" he said pawing at the card.

"Well, let's make some anyways. Maybe we'll find the magic ingredient later on."

After mixing the cookies, you put some away in a little bag and put it in your pocket. Just as you turn to leave, you notice something sticking out from behind one of the posters. It was a secret map in the forest. It led to an orange colored circle in the middle of the map. What could this mean? It's peaked your curiosity. Maybe the stable hand knows about the forest trails.

Lesson 5: Quiz

STOP! Knowing how to properly feed a horse will help him be happier, healthier and you can decrease the chances of sickness. It could be devastating to continue without testing your knowledge each unit.
Do the Quiz for Unit 6.

Watch Video #7 and Read along
Lesson 1: Pasture

"Glad you made it back from the feed shed, this wind is getting dangerous!" the stable hand hollered, "Now help me get these horses inside where we can keep them out of flying debris outside. Oh, and make sure everyone is safe in the stables and out in the pastures!"

> **Read Chapter Seven in the book titled, "Horses!"**

Fill in the blanks with the following words:

HOLES   AREA   FOOD   FENCE   WATER   EXERCISE

All horses need _____. They need a safe _____ that is big enough to run around in. There should not be any _____ or obstacles that a horse could get hurt on. A safe, strong _____ is very important to a keeping a horse. A horse needs plenty of clean, fresh _____ and _____!

Shelters versus Stalls: draw a line to what each protects horses from.
Hint: Some may go to both the shelter and the stall.

PREDATORS

RAIN

SHELTER   BUGS   **STALL in a stable**

in a pasture   SUN

SNOW

WIND

ANGRY KITTENS (just kidding)

Lesson 2: Stables

Mystery Stalls – Read the clues and fill in every square with a ☑ or a ☒ to find out which horse likes which <u>stall</u>, which <u>bedding</u> and how they are <u>watered</u>. Each option can be used only once.

	Pail	Electrical Bowl	Straw	Wood Shavings	Box Stall	Tie Stall
Star	X	√				
Merry Legs	√	X				

Detective Clues:
Clue #1: Star will not drink from a water pail. *(I did the first one for you.)*
Clue #2: The horse who drinks from an electric water bowl lives in the stall with the wood shavings for bedding.
Clue #3: Straw is used for bedding in the box stall only.

Keeping a horse in a stall has its good points and bad points. Decide on each point and draw a line to whether it is good or bad.

HORSE MAY GET BORED

GOOD POINT   PROTECTION FROM PREDATORS

IT IS COOLER IN THE SUMMER

STALL NEEDS TO BE CLEANED

BAD POINT   IT TAKES TIME TO PUT A HORSE IN

PROTECTION FROM BUGS

IT IS WARMER IN THE WINTER

Why should stall doors slide or open outwards? Think carefully about what would happen if the horse was lying down in the stall.

_____

_____

What is wrong with the pictures below? (One thing in each picture)

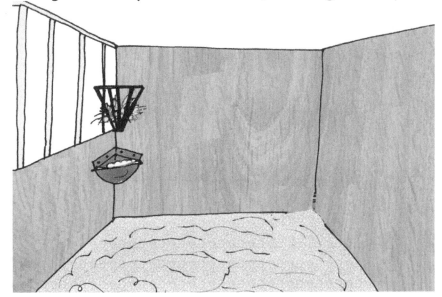

Hint: Check the stall to see what things it <u>must</u> have and then you can figure out what it is missing. Note: A horse needs only one way of being fed and watered.

Hint: There is more to this picture than one would expect!

Lesson 3: Management

Someone messed with the barn sign. Fill it in so everyone will know what to do.

To do list:

#1: Check the horses __ __ __ __ __   __ __ __!

   2) Check his __ __ __ __ __

   3) Check his __ __ __ __ __ __ __

   4) Check the __ __ __ __ __

   5) Clean __ __ !

What does your horse do during the day?

My horses schedule:

Morning _____

Noon _____

Afternoon _____

Night _____

Lesson 4: Practical Activity – BOX STALLS
Look in each set of boxes. What stall cleaning tool is missing?
SHOVEL   WHEELBARROW   RAKE   PICKER   BROOM

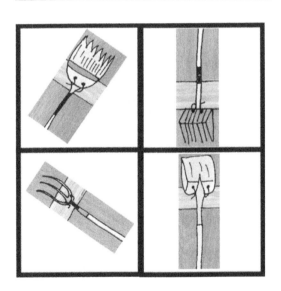

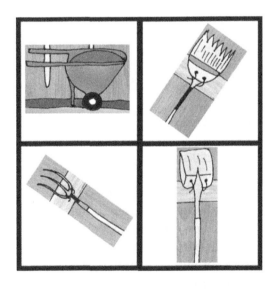

You manage to get all of the horses inside and to keep them safe. Everyone was fed and watered, except one horse did not want to eat or drink. Instead, he hung his head and stood very still, not wanting to move.

"He looks sick," Nickers worried.

"He sure does. Take him over to the health center and I will tend to the rest of the chores."

There's no time for questions now. You decide to rush the horse over to the health center and come back later.

STALL CARD

If you are going to do any traveling or board your horse at someone else's facility, you may want to make a stall card for your horse. This information is important because it lets anyone know all of the important facts about your horse.

Sample Stall Card

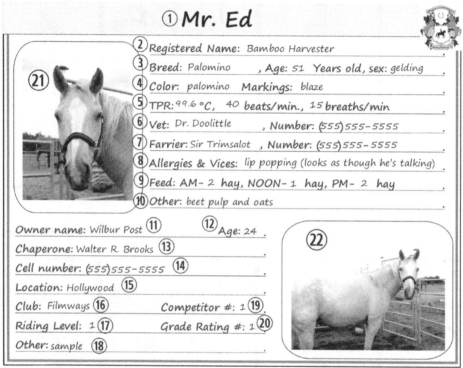

① **Mr. Ed**

② Registered Name: *Bamboo Harvester*

③ Breed: *Palomino*   , Age: *51* Years old, sex: *gelding* .

④ Color: *palomino* Markings: *blaze* .

⑤ TPR: *99.6 °C, 40* beats/min., *15* breaths/min .

⑥ Vet: *Dr. Doolittle*   , Number: *(555) 555-5555* .

⑦ Farrier: *Sir Trimsalot* , Number: *(555) 555-5555* .

⑧ Allergies & Vices: *lip popping (looks as though he's talking)* .

⑨ Feed: AM- *2 hay*, NOON- *1 hay*, PM- *2 hay* .

⑩ Other: *beet pulp and oats* .

Owner name: *Wilbur Post* ⑪   ⑫ Age: *24* .

Chaperone: *Walter R. Brooks* ⑬ .

Cell number: *(555) 555-5555* ⑭ .

Location: *Hollywood* ⑮ .

Club: *Filmways* ⑯   Competitor #: *1* ⑲

Riding Level: *1* ⑰   Grade Rating #: *1* ⑳

Other: *sample* ⑱

Notes on the information:
1. Is the horse's nick name or barn name. This is a name used commonly that the horse should respond to.
2. The horse's registered name is that which is read on his registration papers and used on all legal papers and entry forms.
3. The breed of horse is what the horse most consists of. For example, if he is a Thoroughbred, but also has Quarter horse and Appaloosa in him, put down Thoroughbred 'X'. The 'X' means 'cross'. If the horse is a purebred, just write the breed name. If the horse has unknown breeding, write the word 'grade'. Also on this line is the horse's age, which is self-explanatory. If it is unknown, put a '?'. The last part is asking what sex the horse is. The horse can only be a 'mare', 'gelding' or 'stallion', so write down whatever is appropriate.
4. The horse's color should be your best description possible. See Unit 3 for colors to choose from. Also see markings. Use short form for the left and right legs, which are 'L' and 'R'. Also use 'H' and 'F' for hind and front legs. For example, the right hind leg is 'RH'.
5. 'TPR' is the horse's temperature, pulse and respiration at rest. Temperature is usually recorded in degrees Celsius, the pulse is recorded at heart beats per minute, and the respiration is recorded at breaths per minute.

6. The name and phone number of the horse's regular veterinarian can be vital if the horse's medical background needs to be given when you are not around. Sometimes the owner can become flustered and not remember vital information when in an emergency. Most veterinarian offices use a computer to store data, so the horse's information may be easy to retrieve.

7. Like #6, the same is said for the farrier. He or she may not use a computer to store the horse's information, but he or she may remember the horse and any particulars.

8. Any allergies and bad behavior needs to be recorded so that other people who may be around in an emergency know how to care for your horse, what his usual habits are and what to expect from him.

9. The horse's feeding schedule should also be recorded in case you cannot be there to care for your horse. For example, if you were in a vehicle accident, another person would know immediately what your horse would require.

10. Any other information that may be helpful should be recorded.

11. Your name is important! It is so everyone will know who the horse belongs to.

12. At some places it may be vital to record your information. There are certain rules for juniors at some places. It may even be a deciding factor in where your horse is stalled or what classes you may compete in if you are at an event.

13. If you are a youth and being chaperoned by an adult or parent, you should record this information so that everyone will know who is responsible for you.

14. Make sure to include a phone number that someone would have the least amount of difficulty in reaching you.

15. Write down your address or if you are at an event, write down the name of your hotel and room number, or wherever you are lodging for the night.

16. Your club's name may also affect what events you are in, state it proudly.

17. Your riding level is what group you are in. For example, if you are at a dressage event, you may say 'Training level', or if you are at a pony club event, you may write 'D' level. If you are taking the International Riding Levels you may want to state what level you are currently schooling or testing in, such as 'Junior A' or 'Rider 1' or Equitation.

18. Record any other information you want on this line. It could even be an alternate contact, or your health number.

19. If you are at an event, you may want to record your competitor number. You will be easy to spot if you are wearing your number and someone wants to contact you.

20. Your grade rating can differ from what group you are in. For example, if you are at a pony club event, you may want to record the level you are currently doing book work for. Sometimes the book work, or theory, is not the same as your riding level. You may want to put 'HA' if you are schooling that level. Or you may want to put what grade you are in if you are working on the Academy's Equestrian program.

21. For an easy, visual reference, as well as advertising, put a picture of your horse's front view. Pictures should depict well-groomed horses. An attractive picture will go far in describing how you care for your horse.

22. Again, put a picture of your horse's side view. You may be mounted, but make sure that the horse's body and markings are easy to see. As well, you may want to show off an accomplishment in the picture, such as an award photo would.

You may fill 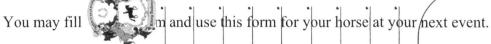 m and use this form for your horse at your next event.

Registered Name:

Breed: , Age: Years old, sex:

Color: Markings:

TPR: °C, beats/min., breaths/min

Vet: , Number: ( ) –

Farrier: , Number: ( ) –

Allergies & Vices:

Feed: AM– hay, NOON– hay, PM– hay

Other:

front picture

side picture

Owner name: Age:

Chaperone:

Cell number: ( ) –

Location:

Club: Competitor #:

Riding Level: Grade Rating #:

Other:

Lesson 5: Quiz

STOP! It could be detrimental to continue without testing your knowledge each unit.
Do the Quiz for Unit 7.

UNIT 8 Health

Watch Video #8 and Read along
Lesson 1: Health & Prevention

the Veterinarian

You took the sick gelding over to the health center.
"Oh, the poor horse, he looks like his happiness level went down too far," the veterinarian said as she surveyed the sick horse. "Let's doctor him up and get him happy again." You stick around to help the sick horse.

Read Chapter Eight in the book titled, "Horses!"

PREVENTION means helping to keep your horse healthy.

Are the following ways good ways of prevention?

Vaccinate your horse – YES   or   NO

Keep a record book for your horse – YES   or   NO

Allow your horse to stay up late – YES   or   NO

Deworm your horse – YES   or   NO

Read your horse a book – YES   or   NO

Sick or Healthy?

Put a check mark if the sign means the horse is healthy.

Put an 'X' if the sign means the horse is sick or hurt.

	1. Alert and happy
	2. Has a cut
	3. Coughing
	4. Diarrhea
	5. Does not want to eat normal
	6. Drooling
	7. Breathes normal
	8. Fever
	9. Lame - limping
	10. Skin is loose and elastic
	11. Has belly pain
	12. Loses too much food when eating
	13. Drinks normally
	14. Bites at belly
	15. Depressed
	16. Really hard dry poop
	17. Shiny coat
	18. Hot hooves
	19. Sweating
	20. Losing weight
	21. Temperature is 37°C
	22. Pees normally
	23. Loss of condition
	24. Behavior has changed
	25. Lays down and then gets up right away

Lesson 2: Ailments

How can you tell if your horse has colic?

1) _____

2) _____

3) _____

Draw a line from the types of wounds to the possible cause.

SCRAPE   Barb wire

TEAR   Nail sticking out

BRUISE   Rubbed raw

CUT   Kicked by a horse

POKE   Piece of glass

If a horse is limping, he may be called LAME.

Circle one.

If the horse is limping with his head low, which leg is sore?

FRONT or BACK

If the horse is limping with his head high, which leg is sore?

FRONT or BACK

Lesson 3: Medicine

What does T.P.R stand for?

1_____

2_____

3_____

Knowing your horse's average TPR is very important. To find the horse's average take it 7 times different days, record it here and then calculate the average.

Horse: _____ * TPR at rest

Day	1	2	3	4	5	6	7	Average
Temperature								
Pulse								
Respiration								

A Vet is a doctor for animals. Vet is short for veterinarian. The vet will check on your horse's health, give needles, give medicine and even operate if necessary.

Should you call a veterinarian? Circle one.

If the horse is sleeping? YES or   NO

If there is an emergency? YES or   NO

If the horse runs away? YES or   NO

If the horse is in distress ? YES or   NO

If the horse is suffering? YES or   NO

If you know what to do? YES or   NO

It is a good idea to have your veterinarian's name and number handy in case of an emergency.

Who is your horse's veterinarian? _____

What is his or her phone number? _____

Lesson 4: Practical Activity

What chaos! The horses did not want to get a needle and broke out of the stalls. Follow their tracks and bring them back to the health clinic. It looks as though the herd split up. Bring back all the horses to the health clinic.

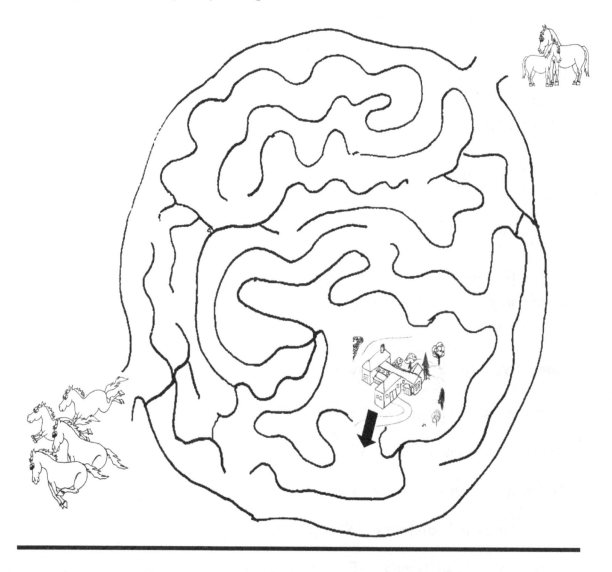

"There, he should feel better by morning," the vet replied with a brilliant smile. "You shouldn't have any more worries. So you're the new apprentice, huh? Glad to formally meet you. If you have any problems, just bring him back to me right away."
"Okay," you tell her politely, glancing through the window, where you could see the forest. A strange glow was coming through the trees.
"There's magic out there you know," she smiled.
"Maybe you could help me with a map I found," you said as you pulled out the folded paper.
"Hrm," she said as she stared intently at it, "I think I've seen it before in the library. If you have a library card, you should check it out there." Then she disappeared into the back room.

Lesson 5: Quiz

STOP! Understanding sickness and knowing how to prevent sickness is not only beneficial to a thankful horse, but also will save you money in vet bills. It would be tragic to continue without testing your knowledge each unit.
Do the Quiz for Unit 8.

"Excuse me, I hate to interrupt, but I wanted to let you know a letter came for you today," the butler announced. "I think it may be important."
You open the letter.

March 1899,

Apprentice,

By the time this letter arrives, I will be gone. I have been summoned by the queen, to do an important quest. Do not let my departure stop your apprenticeship. Quite the contrary, you see, your next quest has already begun. A worthy apprentice knows his Hippology in and out. I expect no less of you.

Trust no one, do not leave your work unattended and guard it with your life. There are many out there who wish to take this information for themselves. They twist it until the truth is no longer there. This has caused a rift in the timeline and we must be careful about the future of the horse. There are not many out there who seek the good of the horse. Keep this ancient knowledge only for other likeminded souls. My dear friend, Podhajsky, said, "We must live for the school. Offer our lives to it. Then, perhaps, little by little, the light will grow from the tiny candle we keep lit here, and the great art—of the haute école—will not be snuffed out." He couldn't have been more correct.

And so I leave you with this quest. Prepare your own lecture on a topic of Hippology and present it to the others.

I trust you will challenge yourself!

You must prepare the 1-3 minute presentation using different visual media, such as posters, diagrams, video, photos, models and other visual aids.

Choose from these topics to study and discuss:

1. Breed – a breed of horse that you have not studied before
2. Discipline – a riding discipline in great detail
3. Arts & Crafts – are you itching to get your hands on some art supplies!
4. Author – for the young horse-lover who is filled with stories of their own
5. Musical – such as drill, pas-de-deux, etc
6. Clinic or event – want to get out of the stall and explore the wonderful world of equestrian around you
7. Driving – don't have your vehicle license? Learn to drive horse and cart instead
8. Therapy – want to help others who are struggling to ride
9. Tack – are you a crafty person who wants to try making some kind of tack
10. Architecture – are you building, aspiring to build something horse related
11. Farrier – are you the kind who wants to care for horses from the hoof up
12. Vet – or do you want to make sure all horses are happy and healthy
13. Coach – are you desiring to teach others to ride
14. Trainer – are you excited to get training horses to do something new
15. Agility – an obstacle course for horses???
16. Equine Mystery – you decide and surprise me!

P.S. I am afraid there is no workbook for you and you are all on your own for this project. Put your thinking cap on and make me proud young apprentice. Your information will be guarded in the Academy's vaults of knowledge in the library's secret wing.

L.C. Spursnomore

UNIT 9 Safety

Watch Video #9 and Read along
Lesson 1: Rules

You slowly walk the horse back to the stables. The wind was slowing you down as you had to brace with every step. Once inside the stables, you put the horse back in his stall. He started nibbling on some hay. The stable hand was nowhere to be seen. Peaking outside the stables, you see a light on in the lounge. Walking slowly up to the rider's lounge, you enter through the front door.

the Coach

The room was dimly lit, but nice and warm. There were several couches by a fireplace. Nickers hopped to the ground and promptly shook himself like a dog. You glance around the walls and notice several signs and an interesting letter on a small table by the door.

"Who's there?" an elderly cowboy came around the corner. "Oh, you must be that apprentice I was told about!" He noticed I had read the letter. "Oh, that. They always send those out. The want the professor to stop his experiments, but that will never happen!"

"No, of course not! Without his inventions, we wouldn't know what Nickers was saying," he hobbled over to pet the little guy.

"What do you mean?" you question.

"Have a seat," the old coach offered, "Stay and I will tell you about it." The coach went on to describe how the professor was trying to create a machine to enlarge Nickers to the size of a regular horse, however the machine enlarged Nickers brain instead. Now the little horse could communicate and learn. The professor is still working on a machine so Nickers can find his family again. "We just don't have the heart to tell him-" the coach stopped talking abruptly. "What the heck was I talking about again?" You were about to tell him, when he slapped his knee and continued, "That's right, so you're the new apprentice and I need to teach you a few things." And the wise, old coach continued on.

Read Chapter Nine in the book titled, "Horses!"

HORSE MASTER'S PLEDGE

I (your name goes here) _____ promise to treat all horses and other horse people with respect and kindness. I will practice safety and responsibility around horses and horse people at all times. I will be dependable and trustworthy. I will set an example for other horse people to follow.

Color in the horse's vision zones:

Who are in the Safe zone?

Circle who is in the Danger zone

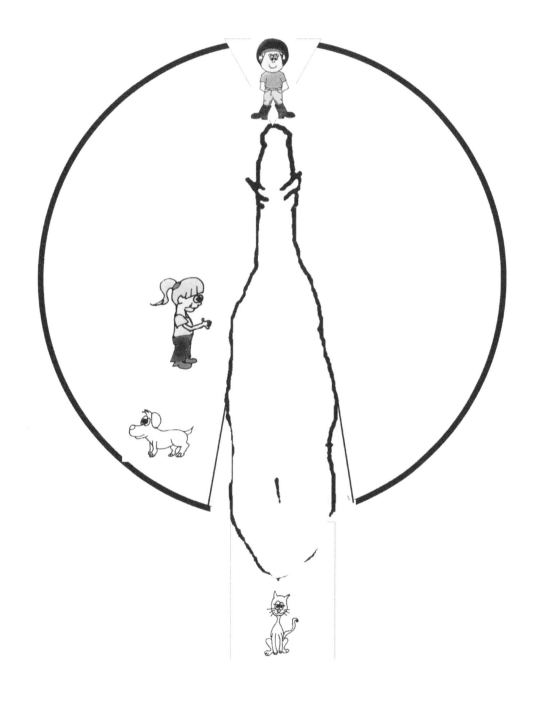

Fill in the blank using these words. Each word is used once. Cross it out after you have used it.

behind   side   gates   safety   watch
softly   sneak   run   pony   scoop   walk   helmet

When meeting or walking up to a horse, approach from the _____.

Be careful if you have to go _____ a horse.

If your _____ poops, you must _____!

Always talk _____ and in a kind voice.

Wear a _____ when riding.

_____, do not _____.

Never _____ up on a horse.

_____ out for others.

_____ first!

Close all _____ .

Circle some things you should NOT go riding with.

HORSE   RIDING PANTS

GUM   BOOTS WITH A HEEL

CANDY   SADDLE

WHIP   BRIDLE

DOG   TOYS

LOOSE CLOTHING

Lesson 2: Apparel

Are these riders ready to ride? If not, explain why. Look in your reference book for Proper Riding Clothes.

_____

_____

_____

_____

Lesson 3: Travelling

This horse is going to go for a trailer ride. Help prepare him. Draw and color a blanket, shipping boots and a halter on the horse.

Lesson 4: Practical Activity

Train the Eye – Can you find which rule is being broken? What will happen if this is not stopped?

_____

_____

_____

The coach talked all through the night. It was morning by the time with finished by saying, "There, now you head on back to the stables and seek out the groom. She'll help show you how to groom your horse and you can get some riding in!"
Nickers jumped into your pocket and you were so excited about being able to ride, you forgot to ask him about what he forgot he was really talking about.

Lesson 5: Quiz

STOP! Being safe around horses is absolutely necessary. It would be ill-fated to continue without testing your knowledge each unit. Do the Quiz for Unit 9.

UNIT 10 Grooming

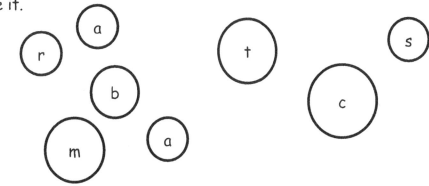
the Groom

Watch Video #10 and Read along
Lesson 1: Basic Grooming
You head back to the stables where a very short lady was waiting, whistling as she was grooming a horse on the cross-ties. "Ah, there you are! It's time to get this horse groomed. The trainer is waiting for you in the riding hall." She busily danced around this way and that way, and it seemed like she didn't know what she was doing, but she did. "Let's first see if you know what to do."

Read Chapter Ten in the book titled, "Horses!"

Bubble bath: Take the letters in the bubbles and use them in the words below. Each letter can only be used once. Color each bubble after you use it.

i   r   a   t   s
k   b   c
m   a

3 reasons to groom your horse are:
1. Keep clean and co__for__a__le.
2. Prevents __o__es.
3. Make s__in and __oat healthy.

It's a good time to groom:
1. D __ily
2. Before and __fter each ride.
3. If the horse is d __ rty.

© 2021 International Riding Academy

The groom chattered on, "That's fantastic! Now, grab that grooming kit over there and let's get busy!"

As you reach for the box, it toppled out of your hands and the contents went flying everywhere. The groom screamed as brushes and hoof picks flew past her head. "I can't believe that didn't hit my eye," she said as she sat on the floor of the barn and rubbed her eye.

"I'm so sorry! Don't worry, I will clean it up," you promise as you immediately squat down to pick up all of the grooming supplies.

Organize the grooming supplies by drawing a line to the correct name.

PAIL   HOOF PICK   RUBBER CURRY   DANDY BRUSH

MANE COMB   SPONGE   SWEAT SCRAPER

Lesson 2: Conditioning

Put these pictures in the proper order of grooming.

Circle the areas that need trimming. If the horse didn't get trimmed, how hairy would he be? Can you make him hairy?

78

Lesson 3: Turn-out

Before this horse can go to a show, he will need a bath. Put the pictures in order and describe what is happening in the pictures.

Number ____

_____

Number ____

_____

Number _____

Number _____

Lesson 4: Practical Activity - Mad Lib Story

Answer these questions before reading the story.

1. Funny name _____   7. A color _____

2. Nonsense word _____   8. A disliked food_____

3. Your name _____   9. An awful drink _____

4. Your favorite sport _____   10. A funny word _____

5. A food_____   11. A game _____

6. A grooming tool _____
_____

Now, let us read the story:

Once upon a time, there was a horse named 1._____, which lived on a ranch named 2._____. The horse was owned by 3._____, who loved to go to shows and play 4._____. In fact, they were going to a show today! That was until 3._____ looked out the window and saw her horse rolling in 5._____.

3._____ ran outside and used the 6. _____ to groom him off but he was still 7._____! So he/she got some 8._____ and mixed it with 9. _____ and scrubbed the pony down.

When he was finally clean, the pony said 11._____ and together they went off to play some 12._____ before the show.

_____

You saw that the groom was too short to reach one of the grooming totes on a high shelf and offered her some help. Grabbing a stool, you climbed up and reach it for her. She quickly walked away still chattering incessantly about proper grooming. You turned to climb back down the stool, but noticed a dusty letter that was hidden under the tote. It said "Gate Keeper Code" and written on the back was -

"Now, don't waste any more time! The trainer is a very busy person. Now, off you go to that big indoor arena over there." She pointed to a grand building. You tuck the letter in your pocket and decide to look at it later.

Make sure you have a proper grooming kit put together and you know how to groom the horse.

Lesson 5: Quiz

STOP! A well-groomed horse is more comfortable and healthier. It would be unfavorable to continue without testing your knowledge each unit.
Do the Quiz for Unit 10.

UNIT 11 Handling

Watch Video #11 and Read along
Lesson 1: Catching

You lead the smart looking mare over to the riding hall, which was an indoor, riding arena. It was elegant in its design, with white walls, wood wainscoting, and large candelabra light. High on the walls were several paintings on every wall and the academy logo at the end wall. Mirrors decorate the end wall as well. You could easily watch yourself ride.

"What took you so long? You kids are all alike nowadays. Never mind, next time you will have to work faster," the trainer scolded as he approached. "Let's go through some things first."

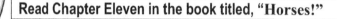

> **Read Chapter Eleven in the book titled, "Horses!"**

When leading a horse circle if it is something you should do and put an x over the things you should not do.

Use a lead rope to lead a pony.

Use a halter to lead a horse.

Lead from the horse's left side.

Lead from the horse's right side.

Hold the rope at the end only.

Hold the rope about 6 inches down from the snap.

Coil the rest of the rope in your left hand.

Coil the rest of the rope in your right hand.

Never coil the rope!

Fan the rope in your left hand.

Lesson 2: Tacking

Good idea or bad idea? Circle one.

1. Going to catch your horse and taking some treats into a herd of horses.

    GOOD IDEA or BAD IDEA

2. Tying a horse with a flat, web lunge line.

    GOOD IDEA or BAD IDEA

3. Tying the horse with about 18-24 inches of free rope.

    GOOD IDEA or BAD IDEA

4. Tying the horse using the cross-ties.

    GOOD IDEA or BAD IDEA

5. Putting the bridle on before the saddle.

    GOOD IDEA or BAD IDEA

6. Tightening the girth slowly.

    GOOD IDEA or BAD IDEA

Lesson 3: Warm-Up

NAME THAT THING !
Fill in the blank squares with the missing letters to see if you can solve the puzzle.
Hint: What should you do with the English stirrups?

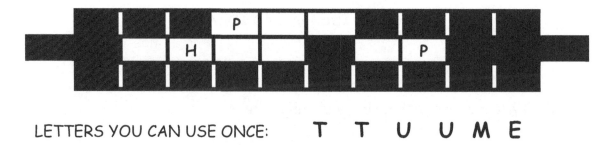

LETTERS YOU CAN USE ONCE: T   T   U   U   M   E

PUT YOUR THINKING CAP ON!
Put these in the order of which they should be done with your horse:

_____ Saddle him

_3_ Groom him down

_1_ Catch him and put a halter on him

_____ Bridle him

_2_ Tie him to something solid

_____ Jog him and tighten the girth

_____ Mount up and ride

Lesson 4: Practical Activity – Round Pen Words?

Follow the letters to spell a word, but which letter starts the word?

_____

_____

_____

_____

Practice tying the quick-release knot

When the trainer was done working with you and the horse, you asked if you could ride through the forest trails. He quickly replied, "Heck, no! You gotta practice your riding skills outside first. Head out to the outdoor arena and do your testing before your allowed in the woods." Glancing up at the paintings you see that the paintings are labeled. For some reason, all of the say the same thing- "the Gate Keeper"– but each had different codes beside them.

"What do all these paintings mean?" you ask the trainer.

"I don't know," he replied, "Best to look them up in the library. That's all I know." He disappeared out the door and was gone.

Lesson 5: Quiz

STOP! Horse handling is no easy task, unless you know what you are doing. It would be unsafe to continue without testing your knowledge each unit.
Do the Quiz for Unit 11.

UNIT 12 Riding

Watch Video #12 and Read along

Lesson 1: Moving

Luckily, the weather was clear enough to head over to the outdoor arena. You decide to save the gate keeper business for later, when you have time to look it up on the computer.

The outdoor arena had a perfectly trimmed hedge around it and letters placed every so often. The riding instructor was standing in the middle, arms crossed, tapping his foot and looking at his watch. You best hurry in.

"That horse is too fast for you," he announced.

Trying to stand a little taller, you mount up in the saddle. "But, I can ride," you say proudly.

He smiled and said, "Prove it."

Read Chapter Twelve in the book titled, "Horses!"

the Instructor

What are 3 things you should do before mounting?

1 _____

2 _____

3 _____

Describe how to make your horse walk on.

_____

_____

_____

_____

_____

_____

88

Lesson 2: Aids

List 4 types of aids:

1. _____

2. _____

3. _____

4. _____

List 1 artificial aid:

1. _____

How many beats are in the gaits? 2 or 4

1. How many beats are in the walk? _____

2. How many beats are in the trot? _____

Draw a picture of a rider in the half seat and on in the rising seat.

Lesson 3: Etiquette

Match the horsemanship rules on the left to their correct reason on the right.

GOOD HORSEMANSHIP	REASON

GOOD HORSEMANSHIP

A. Walk on which side when leading the horse?

B.

C.

D.

E. When riding with others, how far should you be away from other horses

F. A change from trot to walk is called

REASON

_____ You are going to left

_____ A transition

_____ You are going to turn right

_____ One horse length

_____ The horse's left side

_____ You are going to stop

Lesson 4: Practical Activity

Gymkhana is a speed event where horse and riders compete against each other or the clock, to see who is the fastest. There are numerous patterns. Read through the patterns below and see if you can follow the course. On the next page, draw in the patterns.

> **You will need this activity to complete the quest for the gatekeeper in Unit 13.**

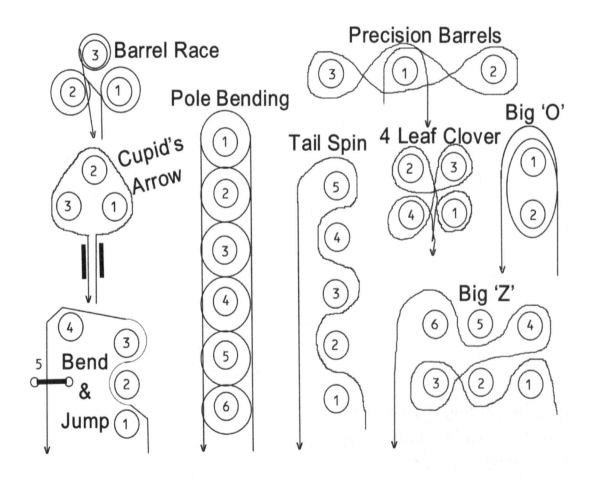

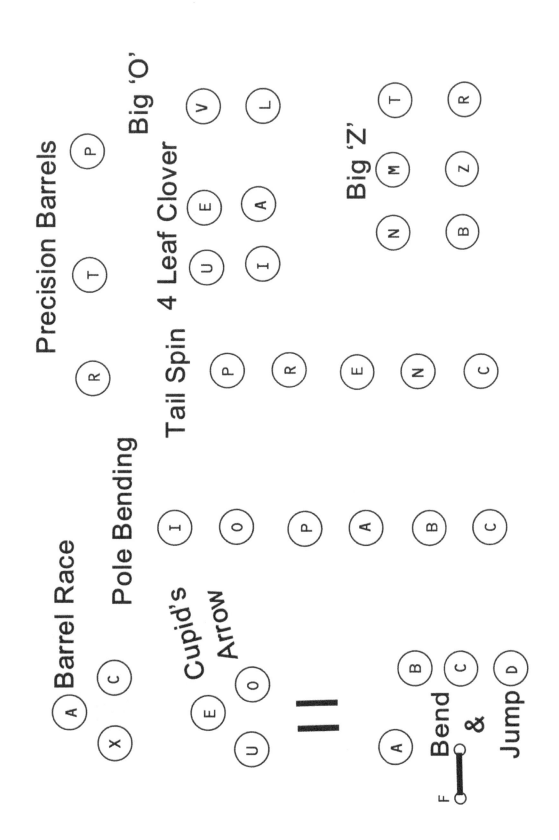

Precision Barrels

Big 'O'

Barrel Race

Pole Bending

4 Leaf Clover

Tail Spin

Cupid's Arrow

Big 'Z'

Bend & Jump

Lesson 5: Quiz

STOP! Riding is safest with a coach, instructor or other expert. It would be catastrophic to continue without testing your knowledge each unit.
Do the Quiz for Unit 12.

After the quiz, the riding instructor looked at you and said, "That's pretty good," he said, "But are you ready for what's out there?" He pointed to the forest. "There is so much more to learn. Classical Horsemanship is the foundation of all riding disciplines. In order to progress with you horse, each horse and rider ride through different levels of progressive training using ménage exercises (riding ring exercises). As the horse and rider go up the levels, the tests get harder. The horse and rider move together in harmony, balance and with grace and beauty. It is like horse ballet, but on horseback! The progressive training is called Dressage. It is done in an arena measured 20 by 40 or 60 meters with letters placed at specific points around the arena. If you wish to learn more, see the International Riding Academy's Dressage program for all of the information, rules, tack, attire, and tips.

For this level the average child can ride in **Classical Walk Trot or higher and start on Young Rider C!** Note, if you are riding in Classical and using a veteran horse (15 years or older), you can choose to ride the veteran tests that are a bit shorter and have optional canter. In order to receiver your rider level, you must canter. You will have to video each test and send it in to the Head Horse Master for viewing. Here is the map. Be careful with them, they are very old. You will have to go on the library computer to look up the instructions. Remember, this is a test of true horsemanship that only you, the young apprentice, can accomplish, if you dare that is...."

Current tests
are found
online

Keep track of all your riding lesson work in the report card for Young Rider A, B, C & D certificates! Exercises are found in the International Pony Camp Manual. Also, you may ride in the Young Rider test A, B, C or D, pending on your riding level. This is done via video, so record away and send it in!

If you plan to go for your Equitation medal, you will need to complete rider levels I to IV. Get the books and watch the video tutorials online. Take special note that if you score 60+% in any level twice, you can earn an award certificate. Points for the horse accrue to earn a stall plate! Testing is also done via video.

Do you get your CERTIFICATE?

CHECK THE ROAD SIGN AND MAKE SURE YOU COMPLETE EVERYTHING!

Gate Keeper Code: for Grade 4

Follow the clues of each gymkhana pattern to spell the name of the Gate Keeper as according to the diagram on page 90.

Clues:

What is the first barrel taken in Barrel Racing? _____

What is the fourth pole taken in Pole Bending? _____

What is the third barrel taken in Precision Barrels?

_____

In the Tail Spin pattern what is the second barrel?

_____

What is the second barrel taken in Cupid's Arrow? _____

What is the bottom barrel in the Big 'O'? _____

What is the fourth barrel in the '4 Leaf Clover'? _____

What is the fourth barrel the 'Bend & Jump'? _____

What is the last barrel in the Big 'Z'? _____

The Gate Keeper's name is

_____

UNIT 13

The wind continued to howl growing with forc
tapped into something!"
"What do you mean?" you holler back
"The time machine seems to have t
opened the door for his laboratory so the
he added, "And it seems as though
"How much worse is it going to
"I don't know, but we have to
have the sonic oscillator?
him the tool and w

It seems as though these pages have been ripped out! If you are a registered student, contact the head horse master for the lost pages.

The Butler hands you this note.

Dear professor,

I have managed to find a sacred vortex in the Fountain of Youth in Bimini. Legend says that if you follow the Bimini road, it will take you to a continent called Atlantis, a place of superior beings, wondrous technology and impeccable horsemanship. Unfortunately, I got caught in the Bermuda triangle and came out somewhere in the heart of the Amazon jungle. Please, send help. I will make my way through the jungle. Wish me luck and hope to see you soon!

P.S. There is a place of crystal buildings on the edge of a lake, rumored to be the city of the Gods. It is called Puno. Maybe they can help me.

L.C. Spursnomore

Thanks

for being in my camp!

_____

_____

_____

_____

_____

Next time you should register in

_____

Coach/Instructor _____

Camp _____

Date _____

International Riding Academy

Young Rider Program:

A	1
B	2
C	3
D	4

The Young Rider program makes sure your kids are horse smart!

The academy works to prevent accidents and horse-related injury through its training programs, Pony Camps, Young Rider levels, International Rider levels, Classical Dressage, English Performance, Hunter Jumper, Western Performance, Working Equitation and Recreation. The academy also certifies Coaches, Horse Trainers and Stable Managers as well as has diploma programs for Equine Science and many different awards programs.

Be sure to have your coach or instructor send in the form for you to receive your certificate.

Young Rider Program

RIDER

PROGRESS REPORT

NAME
_____

I.R.A. Identification Number
_____

International Riding Academy

Hippology Society

* This program is meant to accompany the Pony Camp program

YOUNG RIDER A - Video Young Rider Test A

Core Concept Demonstrations
- [ ] Barn Rules, Horse's Vision & Blind Spots
- [ ] Approach a horse when tied
- [ ] Give a treat (mindful of teeth)
- [ ] Yield the horse on the ground when tied
- [ ] Use the cross-ties
- [ ] Curry and Dandy brushing
- [ ] Find center using the physio-ball
- [ ] Find contact & balance standing- hold reins
- [ ] Find contact & balance trampoline-hold reins
- [ ] Emergency Dismount "Squirrel"

Rider Calisthenics (Exercises)
- [ ] Ground Stretches
- [ ] Ankle Rotations, Down & Up
- [ ] Arms in Front & Back
- [ ] Airplane Rotations
- [ ] Shift Weight to Balance Saddle

Technical Components
- [ ] Mount using a mounting block or leg (both)
- [ ] Verbal aids
- [ ] Leisure Walk & Working Walk
- [ ] Happy Walk (End of ride)
- [ ] Trot on Lunge briefly
- [ ] Direct Reining
- [ ] No stirrups at walk

Arena Exercises (Dressage arena letters)
- [ ] Pick-a-Point
- [ ] Sit'n'Soak
- [ ] Anywhere Anytime
- [ ] Ride the Rail
- [ ] Half Arena Walk
- [ ] La Smircles
- [ ] Little Mulberry Bush
- [ ] Little Whoa-Go-Whoa-Go Monster
- [ ] Railway Tracks
- [ ] Walk the Line
- [ ] 'X' Marks the Spot
- [ ] Walk Over & Change Rein
- [ ] Chase Person or Thing on Foot (Walking)
- [ ] Boots on Post Game (with help)

YOUNG RIDER B - Video Young Rider Test B

Core Concept Demonstrations
- [ ] Approach & catch a horse in a pen
- [ ] Lead horse left, right, stop and go

Rider Calisthenics (Exercises)
- [ ] Circles arms forward & backward
- [ ] Knee Lifts
- [ ] Head Rotations

Technical Components
- [ ] Change Rein – Turn around or Diagonal
- [ ] Open Reining
- [ ] Leg Aids
- [ ] Trot (lunge) Stand 2 beats
- [ ] Trot (lunge) post briefly
- [ ] Loose Rein on diagonals at walk

Arena Exercises
- [ ] Around the Clock
- [ ] Spiral In & Out
- [ ] Deep in the Corner Pocket
- [ ] The Clover Leaf
- [ ] Square Clover Leaf
- [ ] Mulberry Bush
- [ ] Figure Eight
- [ ] Oval Energy
- [ ] Half Arena Trot
- [ ] Trot the Line
- [ ] Drill Lines
- [ ] Walk Over the Middle
- [ ] Walk the Barrels
- [ ] Walk the Poles

YOUNG RIDER C - Video Young Rider Test C

Core Concept Demonstrations
- [ ] Approach & catch a horse in a stall
- [ ] Lead horse through gate
- [ ] Put up stirrups (English)

Rider Calisthenics (Exercises)
- [ ] Legs forward & backward
- [ ] Lean Forward & Backward
- [ ] Elbow circles

Technical Components
- [ ] Long & Low Walk
- [ ] Trot without stirrups- briefly
- [ ] Post to proper diagonal
- [ ] Bareback (can be led)
- [ ] Soccer (use horse to score a goal)

Arena Exercises
- [ ] Trot the Barrels
- [ ] Trot the Poles
- [ ] Halt in a Box
- [ ] Arena Worm
- [ ] Springs
- [ ] Dominoes
- [ ] Crazy Dominoes
- [ ] Monster in the Closet
- [ ] Tiny Slow-Go-Slow-Go Monster
- [ ] Weaving
- [ ] Walk Over the Oval
- [ ] Walk Over the Clock

YOUNG RIDER D - Video Young Rider Test D

Core Concept Demonstrations
- [ ] Approach a Horse in a pasture (& catch)
- [ ] Take off halter in pasture & close gate
- [ ] Pick hooves
- [ ] Saddle and Bridle with assistance
- [ ] Take off bridle and put up (figure 8)
- [ ] Tie with quick release knot & untie
- [ ] Unmounted, lower horse's head
- [ ] Circle horse (lunge briefly)

Rider Calisthenics (Exercises)
- [ ] Touch Toes
- [ ] Calf Stretches
- [ ] Side Saddle
- [ ] Post without stirrups briefly

Technical Components
- [ ] Deep breathing
- [ ] Eyes closed (call which leg is forward)
- [ ] Ask for a Free Walk
- [ ] Start Turn on Forehand (up to 1/4 turn)
- [ ] Rein-back 3+ steps
- [ ] Attempt to change posting diagonal

Arena Exercises
- [ ] Trot the Rail
- [ ] Dominoes Rail Trot
- [ ] Circle the Wagons
- [ ] Half Tiny Slow-Go-Slow-Go Monster
- [ ] End Transitions
- [ ] Eight Squared
- [ ] Trot the Drill Lines
- [ ] Weaving the Trot
- [ ] Walk Over the Fan
- [ ] To Post or Not to Post

INTERNATIONAL RIDING ACADEMY
QUIZ SHEET for GRADE 4

Student Name: _____

Directions: Use a pencil to fill in the dot that. Erase any wrong answers. There is only one answer per question.

1. Ⓐ Ⓑ Ⓒ Ⓓ
2. Ⓐ Ⓑ Ⓒ Ⓓ
3. Ⓐ Ⓑ Ⓒ Ⓓ
4. Ⓐ Ⓑ Ⓒ Ⓓ
5. Ⓐ Ⓑ Ⓒ Ⓓ
6. Ⓐ Ⓑ Ⓒ Ⓓ
7. Ⓐ Ⓑ Ⓒ Ⓓ
8. Ⓐ Ⓑ Ⓒ Ⓓ
9. Ⓐ Ⓑ Ⓒ Ⓓ
10. Ⓐ Ⓑ Ⓒ Ⓓ
11. Ⓐ Ⓑ Ⓒ Ⓓ
12. Ⓐ Ⓑ Ⓒ Ⓓ
13. Ⓐ Ⓑ Ⓒ Ⓓ
14. Ⓐ Ⓑ Ⓒ Ⓓ
15. Ⓐ Ⓑ Ⓒ Ⓓ
16. Ⓐ Ⓑ Ⓒ Ⓓ
17. Ⓐ Ⓑ Ⓒ Ⓓ
18. Ⓐ Ⓑ Ⓒ Ⓓ
19. Ⓐ Ⓑ Ⓒ Ⓓ
20. Ⓐ Ⓑ Ⓒ Ⓓ
21. Ⓐ Ⓑ Ⓒ Ⓓ
22. Ⓐ Ⓑ Ⓒ Ⓓ
23. Ⓐ Ⓑ Ⓒ Ⓓ
24. Ⓐ Ⓑ Ⓒ Ⓓ
25. Ⓐ Ⓑ Ⓒ Ⓓ
26. Ⓐ Ⓑ Ⓒ Ⓓ
27. Ⓐ Ⓑ Ⓒ Ⓓ
28. Ⓐ Ⓑ Ⓒ Ⓓ
29. Ⓐ Ⓑ Ⓒ Ⓓ

30. Ⓐ Ⓑ Ⓒ Ⓓ
31. Ⓐ Ⓑ Ⓒ Ⓓ
32. Ⓐ Ⓑ Ⓒ Ⓓ
33. Ⓐ Ⓑ Ⓒ Ⓓ
34. Ⓐ Ⓑ Ⓒ Ⓓ
35. Ⓐ Ⓑ Ⓒ Ⓓ
36. Ⓐ Ⓑ Ⓒ Ⓓ
37. Ⓐ Ⓑ Ⓒ Ⓓ
38. Ⓐ Ⓑ Ⓒ Ⓓ
39. Ⓐ Ⓑ Ⓒ Ⓓ
40. Ⓐ Ⓑ Ⓒ Ⓓ
41. Ⓐ Ⓑ Ⓒ Ⓓ
42. Ⓐ Ⓑ Ⓒ Ⓓ
43. Ⓐ Ⓑ Ⓒ Ⓓ
44. Ⓐ Ⓑ Ⓒ Ⓓ
45. Ⓐ Ⓑ Ⓒ Ⓓ
46. Ⓐ Ⓑ Ⓒ Ⓓ
47. Ⓐ Ⓑ Ⓒ Ⓓ
48. Ⓐ Ⓑ Ⓒ Ⓓ
49. Ⓐ Ⓑ Ⓒ Ⓓ
50. Ⓐ Ⓑ Ⓒ Ⓓ
51. Ⓐ Ⓑ Ⓒ Ⓓ
52. Ⓐ Ⓑ Ⓒ Ⓓ
53. Ⓐ Ⓑ Ⓒ Ⓓ
54. Ⓐ Ⓑ Ⓒ Ⓓ
55. Ⓐ Ⓑ Ⓒ Ⓓ

Total Correct

QUESTS:

1. Number of Horse-related books read? _____

2. Number of hours spent with a horse? _____

3. Type of presentation?
Circle one:
BREEDS DISCIPLINE
AUTHOR   ARTS/CRAFTS
MUSICAL   CLINIC/EVENT
DRIVING   THERAPY
TACK   ARCHITECTURE
FARRIER   VETERINARIAN
COACH TRAINER
MYSTERY

4. Young Rider level completed?
Circle latest level:
   A   **B**   **C**   **D**

_____
Coach's/Instructor's
Signature

Certificate of
ACHIEVEMENT

THEORY AWARD
for completing
GRADE 4
of the Equestrian-4-Kids Program!

_____
Date

_____
Teacher

IV   III   II   I   D   C   B   A

Circle the highest rider level →

← Circle the number of horse books read

Project type

HORSE HAPPINESS LEVEL - Circle the horse as per the number of hours spent with a horse

10   20   30   40   50   60   70   80   90   100

8+   7   6   5   4   3   2   1

Made in United States
North Haven, CT
27 February 2024

49299017R00057